John Wetzlau

Under Both Flags

Romantic Drama in Four Acts

John Wetzlau

Under Both Flags
Romantic Drama in Four Acts

ISBN/EAN: 9783337126728

Printed in Europe, USA, Canada, Australia, Japan

Cover: Foto ©Andreas Hilbeck / pixelio.de

More available books at **www.hansebooks.com**

Under Both Flags.

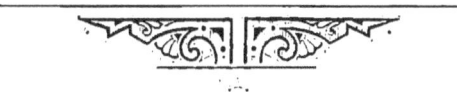

ROMANTIC DRAMA IN FOUR ACTS

......Written by......

JOHN WETZLAU.

SOLE PROPRIETOR, EMIL WETZLAU.

BELLEVILLE, ILL.

Cast of Characters:

MR. WALKER, Planter from Kentucky.

GEORGE, His Son.

MR. WALLWOOD, Planter from South Carolina.

MARIE, His Daughter.

WESTERLAW, Planter.

STEVENS, Planter.

MR. JOHNSTON, Stranger from Baltimore.

General commanding before Petersburg.

Adjutant.

Corporal.

First Soldier.

Second Soldier.

MOTHER SALLY,
WILLIAM, Her Son, } Slaves of Walker.
BALL, Negro Boy,

BEN, } Slaves of Wallwood.
MARK,

FRANK, Negro Slave.

Negroes, Soldiers, Etc.

SCENE PLOT.

ACT I.

An open place. To the left, a dwelling with portico. To right, entrance to garden. In the rear, garden wall partly hidden by trees.

ACT II.

Library with doors on each side. *Change.* Same as Act I.

ACT III.

Room with windows each side centre door.

ACT IV.

Camp. Guns standing in pyramids. Kettles hanging over fire. Soldiers lying around.

SYNOPSIS.

ACT I.

Time of action: Campaign, 1860.

Wallwood and daughter visit Walker. During visit, Wallwood tries to induce Walker to join the Rebel cause, but is met by a prompt refusal. Angered at this, he breaks off all communication with him, and wants his daughter to do the same, but she publicly betrothes herself with Walker's son, George.

ACT II.

Time: Two years later.

Scene at Wallwood's home. He has lost nearly everything, even his blockade-runner Floyd, and is on the verge of ruin. Westerlaw, a planter, asks for his daughter's hand, and Wallwood gives his consent to save himself. Marie refuses him, and in a quarrel defies her father.

Change.

A band of guerillas has attacked a neighbor of Walker's. The latter goes to his rescue, but is nearly killed himself. William, his slave, cuts him out, and is set free with the rest of the slaves on the return. Sally sees the prisoner they have captured, and, recognizing in him the murderer of her parents, shoots him dead.

ACT III.

Time: Two years later.

Wallwood is visited by a stranger from Baltimore, a friend of Booth's, with whom he makes arrangements to murder Lincoln and his Cabinet. George arrives at the plantation in response to a note from Marie, who has been deceived by her father in inviting him. Wallwood, the stranger, and Westerlaw have overpowered George, and are going to lynch him, when the negroes, headed by Ben, set George free and bind the others.

ACT IV.

Time: One year later.

Camp before Petersburg. Wallwood is captured as a spy and sentenced to be shot. Marie, who is visiting George, recognizes him and makes a strong plea for his release. But in vain, and as the shots which execute her father are heard, she falls fainting to the ground.

ACT I.

Scene I.—William and Sally.

William (*winding a wreath*)—Well, this will make a pretty wreath. These red flowers look so well with these greens. The young master will be pleased to find the room decorated, which his bride is to occupy. I wonder how she looks, and if she is as kind as the young master.

Sally (*entering with flowers*)—Well, I have brought still more flowers, almost stripping the whole garden. Hurry up, William, so that we will be able to finish this, otherwise they will surprise us, and spoil our happy plan; therefore, hurry up.

William—O, mother, don't you see how busy I am. I should think one could see by my industry, that it is for my young master, for whom I am winding these wreathes, for I love him above all.

Sally—Yes; and he merits it, too, as well as his father. When one sees how other masters treat their slaves, we cannot thank Heaven enough for our master.

William—That's so. And had we no wish for liberty and self-thought, we would be happy. For our master is good to us, and tries to make up for the crime that his race committed when they forced the chains on us.

Sally—Be quiet, my son. I often enough hear you complain about our fate, while I praise Heaven for it.

William—Give thanks? Give thanks, that we are slaves?

Sally—We are that, certainly. Yet, how easy do we have it under our master.

William—Yes; he is good to us, and I love him as much as you do, but the wish for liberty I cannot, therefore, smother. The young bird leaves its downy nest and travels to foreign countries. Him I would follow to admire Gods, beautiful country outside from these scenes.

Sally—Yes, yes; the world is too narrow for our youth. But the old folks love the soil on which their cradle stood, and like best to shade themselves under the tree they knew as a shrub.

William—That is not always the case. You likewise were not born here, but in South Carolina. Would you wish to return?

Sally—No; the earth where I was born is red with the blood of my parents, and only with terror can I think of my childhood.

Scene II.

Enter Frank, (*carrying a small cask of wine*)—God be with you. My master here sends Mr. Walker a small cask of wine to welcome his guests.

Sally—This will please Mr. Walker very much. Set it down here, Frank.

William—Well, Frank, what's the news?

Frank, (*sorrowfully*)—Hm, news it is, even if it is not good.

William—How so? Tell us!

Frank—You know my brother Tom, who is at Planter Brown's? Now, Marie loves him as he does her. But the overseer has also cast an eye on her, and because she would not submit to him, he made my brother suffer for her refusal. He had him whipped day after day if he committed any mistake or not, so that his wounds had no chance to heal. He ran away, but was soon run down by the dogs. Only yesterday they brought him back. O, God, who can describe his looks. The beasts had torn the flesh from his limbs, but in spite of this he was whipped. Our master had us driven there, so that we should take an example at this devilish act. My poor brother, Tom!

Sally—Be quiet! Be quiet! You stir up old wounds.

Frank—Does the story excite your fears already? You ought to have seen my poor brother yourself, and hear his screams of pain. But no mercy was shown him. They beat and beat until his senseless form fell to the ground.

Sally (*staring in front of herself*)—O, father, I see your bloody corpse.

Frank—How, Mother Sally? Your father?

Sally—Died under the lash for the same cause.

Frank—What? Mr. Walker did——

Sally—Walker; do not wrong this man, who was an angel to me. I was born in South Carolina, on the plantation of a devil named Stevens. In the same manner as your brother Tom, my father was persecuted until he ran away. He was captured with the aid of the dogs, and dragged fainting into the yard. In vain did my mother pray in the dust before him; in vain did I clasp my hands round Stevens' knees. With his foot he spurned me from himself, and shouted: "Give me the whip! I will drive these fainting fits out of the dog," and applied the lash, though the blood squirted towards him with every blow, and beat, when my father was already a corpse. My mother fell fainting upon the dead body of her husband, and when she came to, they tore her away from the corpse, a raving maniac. O, this fearful laughter still quakes through my soul.

William—No farther, mother. Spare yourself.

Sally—Do you believe, the pain gives way when the tongue is silent?

Frank—Go on, Mother Sally, your grief is balm for mine.

Sally—My mother became quieter. No complaint again passed her lips. Not a tear rolled from her staring, sunken eyes. No watch was kept upon her movements, and if so, a very irregular one. All thought that she had been restored to her senses. One night a horrible cry awoke us from our sleep. I jumped up, and ran to the bed of my mother; it was empty. I tore open the door of our hut. O, God, what a sight struck my eyes. The manor was in flames, and on its roof stood my demented mother, a burning torch in her hand. She was laughing, that a cold chill ran down my back. "Stevens," she cried, "you murderer of my husband, you, I curse, and as true as your house, eaten up by these flames, will crumble in ashes, just so true, if there be a righteous God in the Heavens above, will you fall as a victim at the hands of my child." The building caved in, burying my afflicted mother under its smoldering ruins. (*Covers her face with both hands.*)

Frank—Horrible!

William—Why am I not free, so that I might undertake your revenge?

Sally—Be calm, my son; think not of revenge. If God will fulfill the curse of my mother, he will so decree; it is in His power. I crave for no revenge.

Frank—Poor Sally; how came you to leave the villian, and fall into the hands of that kind Walker?

Sally—I was still a child, about ten years of age, when I lost my parents, and still did grief tug at my young life. I was not sick, yet, every day I felt nearer the grave. Stevens kept out of my way; was it his conscience, was it my peaked face, or was it the curse of my mother, that filled him with terror of me, I cannot tell. One day, Mr. Walker, who was traveling through the neighborhood, stopped in, and happened to notice me crying on the hill under which they had hastily buried my father. He stopped and asked me if I was sick, and why I cried. His kindness awakened my confidence in him, and sobbingly I told him of the fate of my parents. He was touched, for in vain did he try to hide a tear from me; this interest, this sympathy for a poor, orphaned negro child. O, who can tell, what took place within me; my grief was broken and for the first time did I feel that I was a creature of God.

Frank—Well, and Mr. Walker?

Sally—Asked me if I would like to go with him. Heaven itself lay in this question for me. The future was smiling kindly to me. I had no words of thanks, but took his hand and wet it with tears. He went to Stevens, who was glad to make the sale. In an hour's time, I left the plantation with my new master.

Frank—Here you met a different class of people, for Mr. Walker is known on all plantations, as a kind and noble man.

Sally—I became satisfied with my fate; here is where I found what I had never known before—kind treatment!

Frank—Yes, yes; I was often surprised, when I was here, to see both Mr. Walker and his son treat you like a member of the family.

William—The young master calls you mother, like I do.

Sally—He lost his own when yet a mere child. With my love I tried to make amends. He grew to manhood under my care.

Frank—Yet, I cannot understand, when I see your calmness, that such a terrible past lies behind you.

Sally—Be satisfied; then also will calmness come unto you.

Frank—Calmness! With me? No! I have not the inherited revenge of a mother, but the revenge of my whole race. And, by God, if I can cool it——

Sally—Fie! Who has such thoughts? For such thoughts bring misfortune. He, who thinks of revenge, offends God, for He alone is judge.

Frank—Then we are worse than the beast, which can revenge itself with its teeth, its claws. Are we not at the mercy of every passion? Are we protected by religion? Are laws framed for us? Are we not dependent upon ourselves? If my whole race thought as I did, we would wade through blood either to liberty or to the gallows. If I become able to revenge my brother's disgrace, I swear——

Sally—Go, young man, and tame this fury, that will otherwise ruin you. Ask God to temper your feelings (*takes the flowers*). Now, go, Frank; your long stay may bring you punishment. [*Exit into house.*

Frank—I will jump over the fence, and take a short cut. Will your master stay away long?

William—I don't know; he and his son drove to the station to meet a Mr. Wallwood and daughter, who come to pay us a visit. We have bound wreaths to decorate the young lady's room.

Frank—Yes; we wind flowers for them, they thorns for us; may God change it. Good-bye, William; will you pay my poor brother Tom a visit next Sunday, if he is still alive?

William (*giving him his hand*)—I will certainly come; I will ask my master to allow me to bring him something strengthening.

Frank—Yes, you are a friend, and stick to your race. I am certain that we may depend upon you, if anything turns up.

William—Maybe, not as you mean. I will not offer my hand to rebellion.

Frank—You could deny your race, because you have it better than we?

William—I feel your misfortune, as well as mine; I miss liberty, as well as you, and my whole race does. But, can I wrong my mother? Could I reward the man, who has always been kind to me, with a bad act? And is it not craziness what you are plotting? Where are you free in America?

Frank—In Canada!

William—Have you wings? Only then can you get there. Take an example at your brother. Go, and greet the others; and, like my mother, do I beg you to have patience.

Frank—Patience! Patience! Poor Tom! How well do I see, that there is no help for us. [*Exit.*

William (*alone*)—The poor bear much. God give them strength!

Scene III.—William; Sally comes out of the house.

Sally—Hurry up, William, the wagon is crossing the bridge. Run! Open the gate!

William—Back so soon; they drove very fast. [*Exit.*

Sally (*alone*)—Thank God, the room is in order. It was high time. It will please the young master, when he sees the room of his bride so beautifully decorated. I did what I could to make her entry into this house a pleasant one. God will, that it lead to happiness. Here is this cask of wine, which Frank brought. Hm, that ought to have been carried into the cellar. Hm, nothing but the fate of poor Tom made William forget to put it away. No wonder, did it not worry me so, that I again lived through the terrors of my childhood, and tears came to those old eyes. O, Heavenly Father, how many sacrifices from your race will this country yet demand?

Scene IV.—Sally; Walker; Wallwood; George, leading Marie; William, following.

Walker—Welcome, Mr. Wallwood; welcome, young lady; and may your stay here be a pleasant one. Ho! William, take care of the horses, and bring the trunks into the rooms intended for our guests. [*Exit William.*] Well, Mother Sally, how fares the kitchen? Have you provided for us?

Sally—I hope, sir, that you will be satisfied, if you have but a little patience. It is not yet quite ten o'clock.

Walker—We have driven very fast then.

Wallwood—This delay is just to my liking, as we breakfasted at the last station.

Walker—Well, may I ask you to enter the house, and make yourself at home.

Wallwood—How would it be to remain out here in the open air. The air is delightful, and the trees give sufficient shade.

Walker—As you wish it; and, young lady, if you are also satisfied, I beg to remove your wraps.

Marie—With pleasure, if you will allow me.

George—I beg you to entrust me with your hat and shawl.

Marie—Do you know how to take care of such delicate things?

George—I will concentrate my whole attention upon it; I know, such things are looked upon as sacred by the ladies.

Marie—Certainly, as with the men, snuff-box and cigars. (*Hands him hat and shawl.*) Well, who will catch hold of a hat in such a manner? You are spoiling the bouquet.

George—Aha, now, I've got the right place. A person always learns more and more.

Sally (*wants to take the things*)—Will you allow me, young master?

George—O, Mother Sally, what are you thinking of. Leave such a weighty matter to profane hands.

Marie (*laughing*)—I hope you will place a guard over them.

George—At least, lock and key shall guard them.

[*Exit into house.*

Walker—Young lady, we beg for your company.

(*Sally placing chair for her.*)

Marie—No, you good soul, bring me that chair.

(*Sally does it.*)

Walker—Aha; this one will be reserved for the custodion of the hat!

Marie—Not more than right; he, who takes care of our finery, shall not be forgotten.

George (*comes back*)—Now, that is finished and done away with.

Marie—As an expression of my thanks, stands this chair for you; rest yourself after your hardship.

George—And sun myself in the mild rays? Immediately.

Sally (*nudging him*)—Young master, a word with you.

George (*going to her*)—Well, what do you wish, Mother Sally?

Sally (*whispering*)—Why don't you show the young lady her room? I decorated it a little, and would like to have her see it before the flowers become withered.

George—Ah! See! That's what I call mindfulness! Well, well, we will take a look at it.

Marie—What secrets have you there?

George (*sitting down*)—We are engaged in a conspiracy.

Marie—It appears so.

Sally (*to Walker*)—Mr. Harley sent a small cask of wine, and, as he said, to welcome the guests.

Walker—Well, that was good of him. It reminds me, too, that we are sitting here without a drink. William, bring up a few bottles out of the cellar. Then you can bottle off this cask. Friend Harley keeps a good brand. [*Exit Sally into house.*

Walker—Now, young people, do not speak with the eyes only, as we two have long ago forgotten that language. Set your tongues into motion, so that we may also be able to take part in your conversation.

George—The tongue generally is silent when the eye is so agreeably occupied.

Wallwood—Enough of this! Tell me, Marie, how do you like this part of the country?

Walker—You ask this question too soon, for now that rogue, Cupid, is sitting on every blade.

Marie—And without Cupid, this place pleases me.

Walker—This region will merit your thanks, if you make the same remark in two years from now.

George—You have not seen much of Kentucky yet; your trip was short and rapid.

Marie—But I was pleased with what I did see.

Wallwood—Yes; the soil is good; the plantations all look well. One can see that wealth reigns here. How many head have you?

Walker—I do not understand you.

Wallwood—I mean, how much black property have you?

Walker—O, yes; I have thirty negroes.

Wallwood—Hm, not very much; still, a living can be made from them if they are worked judiciously.

Walker—I have more than I need; I am not seeking a fortune.

Wallwood—That is wrong! Each must strive to gain riches. For he, who has wealth, may speak; only he, who has money, is in the right.

Walker—Those are not exactly my sentiments.

Wallwood—You should prepare for the future; buy more negroes, now, while they are still cheap; soon, we may have to pay twice the amount.

Walker—I believe, that they will soon drop to zero, as the latest move in political circles seems to indicate.

Wallwood—Explain yourself.

Walker—Well, I believe, that the whole institution will soon fall out with the spirit of the times.

Wallwood—We'll see about that; we will see, if we can't muzzle this spirit.

Walker—I wish you luck to your undertaking.

Marie—If our fathers are getting into politics, we might as well leave them to themselves.

George—You're right! Come, and I will show you your room.

[*Enter William, bringing wine and glasses.*

Walker—Stay, children! We will drop politics.

Wallwood—Pshaw! Let them go, so that we can at least have a sensible conversation.

Marie—Which is impossible in our presence, I suppose? We thank you!

Walker—Hold! First take a glass of wine.

[*William fills the glasses; then takes up cask and walks into the house.*

Walker—Wallwood, touch glasses for good friendship. Young lady, I drink to your health, and may you always feel as well and happy here, as your heart may wish.

George—And may your feelings towards me never change from what they are to-day, is my wish.

Marie—And that I may always occupy that position in your heart, which your love has awarded me, is my wish and ambition. [*All touch glasses and drink.*

Wallwood—Enough! Enough! Betake yourselves away!

Marie—Papa! I see the change of air has not affected your gallantry!

George—Come, Marie, I will show you through the park.

Marie—When we will walk on roses.

George—Could I but strew your path through life with roses!

Marie—Still, there would be many thorns. [*Exit arm in arm.*

Wallwood—Thank God! The air is cleared. Now, we can talk business.

Walker—Business? What kind of business?

Wallwood—You see, I am very thorough in all matters, and class every event as business. When, about four years ago, your son was traveling through South Carolina, he, on the strength of a previous acquaintance, paid me a visit. Although I barely remembered your name, I gave him a most cordial welcome. Don't be offended, as it is thirty years since we accidentally met in Washington.

Walker—It undoubtedly is so long ago. Well? And——

Wallwood—I soon noticed that both he and my daughter were struck with each other; I did not interfere, and acted as if I noticed nothing. After he left, a constant correspondence sprang up; letters being received and sent off daily. A few weeks ago, he asked for my daughter's hand. He was accepted; that is, conditionally, and I made up my mind to journey hither. As the saying goes, "what the eye sees, the heart is compelled to believe."

Walker—If you mean in regards to my son's character, I can vouch for that.

Wallwood—Character! Fudge! He is a gentleman like you and I; that signifies little!

Walker—I thought, that character was a——

Wallwood—Secondary matter! With me, possession is what counts.

Walker—As to that, I am not poor; my son is my sole heir.

Wallwood—What do you call not being poor?

Walker—You get at the matter thoroughly.

Wallwood (*who is re-filling and emptying his glass in the meantime*)—That is my motto.

Walker—Well, my property is free from debt, besides which I have $20,000.00 cash.

Wallwood—Hm, that will do for the start. The young people must see to it, that they advance. And, when do you propose to turn all over to your son?

Walker—Turn it over? What belongs to me, belongs to him without my formally turning it over to him.

Wallwood—Well, that will have to do for the present; I have another reason for speaking with you, but we will put that off till later. I will give my daughter——

Walker—Have I asked you, what you are going to give her?

Wallwood—That is unnecessary. I will give my daughter nothing direct. What is set aside for her, will be put out on interest. Everything must be taken into consideration.

Walker—Your suspicions are becoming insulting. If you think so badly of my son, as to imagine that he would forget himself so far as to rob his wife of her dowery, why——

Wallwood—I think badly of every one, until I have been convinced of the contrary.

Walker—With me, it is just the opposite.

Wallwood—That's bad for you.

SCENE VII.—Marie, George, Sally.

Marie—My room is beautiful and decorated like a ball-room; shall we return to our fathers, or shall we linger along?

George—I await your commands.

Wallwood—Begone! We are deeply interested in business.

Marie—Business? Well, well! Are you selling out?

Wallwood—Something like it!

George—If that's the case, I should suggest a promenade through the woods.

Marie—I am satisfied. But I would like to cover my head; worthy keeper of the wardrobe, my hat!

George—With or without trimmings?

Marie—You may keep the shawl as a sign of my favor.

George—Very well.   [*Exit into house.*

Marie—Well, Mr. Walker, your son shows good material for a handsome husband. As yet, he obeys every sign and command.

Walker—I believe you; when love commands.

Marie—Love? That's correct, and to it I have sworn, and I will never take a furlough!

Walker—Correct, my child! Man lives but to love.

Wallwood—Man lives but to transmit.

Enter George, with Marie's hat—Here it is, and, as I hope, artistically handled.

Marie—Very good; we will now release our papas from our presence.

Wallwood—I am anxiously awaiting the fact.

Marie—Papa Walker, are all papas as gallant as mine?

Walker—All are, at least, not so outspoken.

Marie—Well, then, I may hope to tarry longer with you in the future.

Walker—You will ever be welcome.

Marie—Enough! The hat is donned; the track is clear; now may the path through life begin!

George (*offering his arm*)—And at your side, one wishes that it may never end! [*Both exit.*

SCENE VIII. Wallwood; Walker.

Wallwood (*looking after them*)—That you would chatter till you turned black in the face!

Walker—That is the golden dream of youth; we have also dreamt it.

Wallwood—Not I; I only thought of the real; I never bothered about dreams.

Walker—Then you have denied yourself the best part of your life.

Wallwood—Fudge! Stuff! But now to more important matters! A time is coming, that demands serious thought.

Walker—Do you mean the presidential election?

Wallwood—Yes. The South is too weak. Our friends in the North are disrupted. As we will not support him, Douglas has no hope. For Breckenridge I fear the same fate, as the supporters of Douglas hate him. Fillmore, as small as the number of his supporters may be, is still one of us, but weakens our cause, against which these damn Republicans stand like a stone wall. What will be done?

Walker—More than likely, they will elect their candidate.

Wallwood—Well? And what then?

Walker—There is nothing for us to do, but submit! The majority rules; that is the law!

Wallwood—Law! Law! And when the law fails to please us, it ceases to be the law!

Walker—Friend! You are seeing visions, which I do not understand.

Wallwood—You will soon understand me. I tell you, great events are in preparation. Great work is being done. If these

Republicans win during the next campaign, South Carolina will secede from the Union. A secret understanding pervades the Southern States, and all will secede with her.

Walker—By God, you surprise me! Are you plotting treason?

Wallwood—Treason! Where can you find treason? Shall we allow ourselves to be despoiled of our rights? Shall we allow our property to be confiscated?

Walker—Who will despoil us of our rights? Who will confiscate our property?

Wallwood—Have they not hindered us in our right by refusing us permission to take our property into Kansas? Has not John Brown shown what they are driving at?

Walker—Shall the Union be responsible for the deeds of the individual? Or, did she hinder you, when you let this same individual die on the gallows?

Wallwood—What do I hear? You are taking sides against me?

Walker—I stand, where I always stood, and where I always will stand; I stand by the law, and the flag of my country!

Wallwood—Were you not interested as we are, I would no longer trust you; but in this case, your own advantage will urge you into our ranks. When we secede, we will have a well-drilled and well-armed army at our disposal, and before the Yankees can arm themselves, we will be masters of Washington!

Walker—I yet hope, that this will not occur. What grounds have you for such a monstrous proceeding?

Wallwood—What grounds? By God, you are no Southerner to ask this question!

Walker—I am a Southerner, and ask this question. The Constitution grants state sovereignty. Within our boundaries we live up to the laws that we frame. The free states themselves deliver up our runaway slaves. What more do you want?

Wallwood—We want the Territories; we want the power; we are in the minority; this must be changed. The South is ordained to rule in this country, and God damn, it shall! You sit in the Legislature! You see, that is the real cause, that brings me here. And to influence you, I sacrifice my child. Work for our plan in the Legislature. It will be an easy matter for you to gain supporters, as our interests are yours also. Kentucky must unite with us!

Walker—And you have elected me to do this? You would make me a traitor? You would have me sully the Constitution, which our fathers have handed down to us? By God! Did I not honor you as a guest, I would speak in another strain.

Wallwood—You stand as an enemy against us!

Walker—He, who is an enemy of my country, is also an enemy of mine. And take my word, I will do what's in my power to shield Kentucky from your treason. And if our State, may God prevent it, should try to stand by you, I would be the first to train the cannons onto the Rebels!

Wallwood—You are a damned Abolitionist!

Walker—I am a citizen of this glorious Republic, and as such, I know my duty! Not the clod, but the United States is our country! And he, who participates in treason against his country; he, who baits citizen against citizen, is more contemptible than he who robs the church.

Wallwood—Ha! And to this brood should I give up my child?

Scene IX.—George; Marie.

Marie—It is becoming exceedingly lively here; has the wine gone to your heads?

Walker (*without noticing her*)—If you insist upon participating in this treason, you will be unable to escape the punishment. You will be unable to shatter the Union, but you will ruin your own happiness. Your teeming fields will be turned into dreary deserts, your cities and villages reduced to ruins, and the blood of thousands, whom you will draw into this struggle, will be put upon your heads.

George—My God, my father!

Marie—What is the matter here?

Wallwood (*pulling her towards him*)—Away from these men, their breath is poisonous!

Walker—Monsters! You would destroy the peace of your country, on account of an institution, which poisons the very air in which it breathes! Look at Russia, the land of darkness, the spirit of the times is breaking its way. And here, in our free country, you would try to hinder its flight?

Wallwood—By God! Had we but you in South Carolina, I would have them lynch you!

Walker—But now you are standing upon my land and soil, upon which you have set foot as my guest, and for this reason you may be thankful that you depart as a free man. Here, William! Hitch up the horses!

Wallwood—Yes; away from this house, in which this confounded abolitionism reigns. The air becomes oppressive.

Walker—This house was not built to harbor traitors!

George—Father! For God's sake! You are destroying my life's happiness!

Walker—You well know, my son, how much to me your happiness is; but, can I obtain it for you, through treason to our country?

George—Who demands this?

Walker—This man, who is stirring up an intercine war! This man, who would make a Rebel of me.

George—How, Wallwood! Do you mean it? Are you thinking of treason?

Wallwood—In the name of the devil, call it what you will! We would have the South free and independent from this infested Union, that spreads its poison across our boundaries.

George—You would disrupt the Union? This grand work of our fathers would you despoil? You would call down on yourself the curse of this and the after-world?

Wallwood—Enough! What need is there to bandy words? We are done with each other forever!

[*Enter Sally at door.*

George—Maybe not as you think! I know how to honor the duties of a child. Go with him, and, if God will, we will meet again.

Marie—Father! Listen to the supplications of my deathly fear. Do not sacrifice your child on account of your thick-headedness. Give myself to him who owns my heart!

Wallwood—Him? Rather to the meanest negro on my plantation!

Marie—I embrace your knee; by my life, by my love to you, I beseech thee, be reconciled, otherwise you break my heart!

Wallwood—Get up! Cursed be each tear that falls on his account!

Marie—O, father! You would not make your child unhappy? Let yourself be mollified!

Wallwood—Mollified! I swear it here, rather would I see you in the grave, than standing at the altar with this man!

Marie—Well, then, and I too swear, and may God forget me if I break this oath, I swear to be true unto death. See here, before your eyes, cruel father, will I engage myself to him with this kiss. (*Kisses him.*)

George—The union of two hearts is sealed! Dare to tear asunder what God and love have united!

Wallwood—Come here, ungrateful child; I will make you regret this hour!

William—The carriage awaits.

Wallwood—Let us be off!

George—Marie, remember your oath.

Marie—Yours in life as in death!

[*George sinks to his father's breast.*

Walker—Courage, poor son, God will aid you.

Wallwood (*grasping his daughter's arm*)—Shall I drag you into the carriage?

Marie—Be strong, George! Remember your betrothed!

Wallwood (*kicking William*)—Away, you black dog; bring us away from this spot! (*Drags his daughter with him.*)

Sally (*in the door-way*)—That is the free America!

ACT II.

SCENE I.—Wallwood's Library in South Carolina; Room with side doors.

Ben (*sneaks in and listens at door*)—She is not in the room; everything is quiet; she must be in the garden. (*Looking out of window.*) Just so; she is walking about with bowed head and wet eyes. Grief seems to be tugging at her heart, but I have never heard her complain. Often, when I saw her so sorrowful, a gleam of pity wanted to steal upon me.—Pity with our oppressors? Ben! Think of your wife and child, and rejoice that these tyrants must also suffer! Is it not the only comfort you have? I was satisfied with scanty meals and hard work, for, after the heat and hard work of the day, came evening, and I was happy in the possession of my wife, my child. But these monsters! What are to them the sorrows of a negro? For money, they will tear the wife from the side of her husband, the child from the breast of the mother. They will laugh at tears, and the complaints will be silenced by the lash. Oh! My wife! My poor child!

SCENE II.—Enter Mark.

Mark—Is the master not here? (*Lays a paper on the table.*)

Ben—He is not yet back from Richmond, where he went yesterday.

Mark—Ah, and in the meantime this paper for him arrives from Richmond.

Ben—Put it down there. (*Carefully.*) Have you been able to find out anything about the war?

Mark—That is impossible in this house; our master is silent, the daughter takes no interest in it, and, if a stranger calls off and on, the master sends us out into the field.

Ben—Yes, they are very careful and keep strict watch on us.

Mark—Tomy, a slave of our neighbor, came over last night and knocked at my door. He was digging trenches in Richmond. While he was there, he sneaked up on two officers and overheard their conversation. New Orleans has been taken, as well as Doneldson and Nashville. The only thing wanted is, that they capture Vicksburg and Port Hudson. We would then be split in half. I do not understand this.

Ben—Keep on! Keep on!

Mark—There is no more to tell. Tomy had to get away, so as not to be discovered. Many of the enemy's prisoners should be kept in Richmond.

Ben—Enemies! Do you call them enemies?

Mark—That is what the master calls them.

Ben—He, who is his enemy, is our friend. No matter what they may say about these Yankees, I know better, what they want. You see, while I was still in North Carolina, I was one day working in the garden. The master and a stranger were walking in the garden, and I heard the stranger say: "These damn Yankees will not rest until the last slave is set free; they would best like to have a negro for President at once." My master at this moment caught sight of me, and tipped his friend the wink. Well, and these same Yankees are now the so-called enemies. Could I only fight in their rank; by God, there would be no braver soldier!

Mark—Not so, Ben; I am satisfied to remain here, since Tomy told me how the prisoners live in Richmond. Even if we have hard work, we get enough to eat and our night's rest. Our master must also clothe us, and we are free Sundays.

Ben—Free! Like the ox in the stable, where the yoke does not bear down on him. O, were I free, as I wish it, you would hear from me.

Mark—You would run away?

Ben—No, but I would revenge myself!

Mark—Revenge yourself? On our master?

Ben—If this one would be sufficient for my revenge, do you think he would yet be alive? No! I could bathe myself in their blood to cool my sorrow! When they tore me away from my wife and child, and sold me into this state, when I heard the screams of my wife, and my heart nearly burst with grief, my strength was kept up by the thought, "You must revenge yourself." Since that time I can think of nothing else. My life is for sale, only, I cannot agree upon the price for which to sell it. Ha! I would like to strike them a blow from which the entire brood would bleed to death!

Mark—Terrible! Go, go! You frighten me!

Ben—Often have I thought of sneaking into Richmond, to set the city on fire, to blow up their magazine, and bury them with myself under the ruins.

Mark—Well, they have taken good care to prevent this. As Tomy told me, not one of us can go unguarded from house to house.

Ben—I will not yet give up hope; the day will come when I will settle my account with them!

Mark—Do not put yourself into danger. That I will be silent, you know. But be secret, even with our people. Now come, the others are already sitting at the table, and I am very hungry.

Ben—Well, go and eat, for you live only to eat!

Mark—I thought everybody did that. As one cannot eat without living, so can no one live without eating. Do not forget to deliver the paper to the master. [*Exit.*

Ben (*alone with the paper*)—If one could only read, one could now find out how matters stand. But they raise us like animals. Only one thing puzzles me, they let us know of the good of religion, they promise us heaven and its joys. Does slavery exist in heaven also? Or, are they not afraid to share their heavenly joys with us? (*Looking out of window.*) The master! He is in a hurry!

SCENE III.—Enter Wallwood.

Wallwood (*suspiciously*)—What are you doing here alone?

Ben—I brought this paper, which Mr. Haid sent from Richmond.

Wallwood—Where is my daughter?

Ben—I saw her in the garden.

Wallwood—Then call her, and betake yourself to work!

Ben (*muttering as he walks off*)—Here's news! If one could but overhear it!

Wallwood (*alone*)—Damned news! New Orleans captured, as well as Nashville and Doneldson; and Siegel, this damned Dutchman, is defeating us in Arkansas. These Yankees, damn it, seem to stamp armies out of the very ground! Their commerce is flourishing, while ours is ruined. Our gold is going to foreign countries, while the value of our paper sinks daily; where will that end? (*Takes paper.*) Only one piece of good news! My ship has successfully run the blockade. Captain Blond is a man after my heart. My steamer "Floyd" is a great ship. (*Reading.*) Theatres! Concerts! Balls! Just keep on dancing, you Yankees! Ah! (*reading.*) Latest dispatches from the seat of war: On the 4th of April, McClellan with 120,000 men landed at Yorktown. Just come on, we will give you a welcome! On the 6th and 7th, bloody fighting at Pittsburg Landing; the Union army under Grant victorious. On the same day, Foote captured the important position, Island No. 10. On the 8th, the blockade-runner "Floyd," Captain Blond, with a cargo of cotton for England, was captured on the high seas by the Weet! My ship, damn it, my ship! Will everything break down over me? My ship! I am ruined! But, courage! Courage! Can nothing be saved?

SCENE IV.—Enter Marie.

Marie—You back already? I did not expect you to-day!

Wallwood—Richmond is not just now the centre of gaiety, where one would make a long stay. Things look dark; the Yankees are giving us a lot of trouble. Our harbors are blockaded; our commerce is ruined.

Marie—O, Walker, how terribly true were your prophesies!

Wallwood—Not a word about this traitor! Damn it, not a word of him! I have spoken a weighty word with the President. This will never do! More spirit must be infused into these affairs. We must spread terror among these Yankees, if we will conquer them.

Marie—God! How much blood has been spilt, and all on account of this egotism?

Wallwood—Egotism! You unthinking child! Do not come to me with the ideas which you have imbibed from those people in Kentucky.

Marie—And should I approve of the fact, that the happiness of millions has been destroyed? That thousands of men have been sacrified, in order that the authority of a few individuals might be established. I could not answer for it before God.

Wallwood—Every war demands its sacrifices. He, who has the entirety in view, cannot spare the individual. And do we spare ourselves? I was a rich man; that is my past. I loaned my money to the government; if we lose, I am ruined. My ship (*shows her the newspaper*), read, is lost. On the high seas did they capture it, and still I stand by our cause. I would not move an inch, even if the Yankees already stood in Richmond.

Marie—Your plantations will become deserts; your cities and villages will be in ruins.

Wallwood—The damned prophesy of that old scoundrel. But, patience! We will yet fulfill it! By his Satanic majesty, I would myself shoulder a musket and place myself in the rank and file, if they would march onto Kentucky, to revenge myself on that brood.

Marie—God will take care to prevent it.

Wallwood—O, yonder scoundrel has still a place in your heart, but, damn it, I will drive him out of it!

Marie—Do not flatter yourself. I have engaged myself to him; I am bound to him with a holy oath. You may break my heart, but you can never break the love within it.

Wallwood—Away! Away! You stain of dishonor on my name. From now on, you will learn to know to me. Your father is dead; now, you will obey your master, Marie.

Marie—A father I have never found in you, as my love has in vain tried to find. My mother long reposes in her grave, and I now stand as an orphan in my young life. I am dependent upon myself only, upon myself and my love. This gives me strength; with it, and within it, I exist. Now storm, and see, if you will be able to break down my strength.

Wallwood—I shall, damn it, and if it be with your life!

Marie—O, God, why do you bind the child to him, whom you refuse the heart of a father? [Exit.

Wallwood (alone)—The devil! But I will get done with you after the more important matters are settled. My ship is lost; so is my wealth. Hold! No one knows of it. Hm, I might still be saved from ruin. But I will have to bestir myself, else all will be over. Who? Horway, hm, the old fox, he will not walk into the trap; he is too careful. Lant? He would be stupid enough, but he has not enough money. To Richmond? That will be useless; they will have received the news. Hm, hm, to whom shall I go? (Looking out of window.) Who comes there? Westerlaw? That is just the man! Some good star must have brought him hither. (Hides paper.) If the devil has not already sent him some Yankee newspaper!

SCENE V.—Enter Westerlaw.

Wallwood (meets him)—Welcome, welcome; my dear Westerlaw!

Westerlaw—How are you, Mr. Wallwood?

Wallwood—Well, friend, what brings you? Good news?

Westerlaw—That is at present somewhat scarce. New Orleans is captured.

Wallwood—I know it; I upbraided Davis yesterday for not defending the Mississippi better. Such an important position for us!

Westerlaw—I cannot reproach him for that; New Orleans was strongly defended. Who in the world ever thought, that the old lion, Farragut, could pass Forts Philip and Jackson? It is the only event of its kind chronicled in history.

Wallwood—That is what Davis thought, and as he said, that he thought they would now be likely to capture Richmond.

Westerlaw—Well, I do not think, that they are so anxious to get into Richmond just yet. But the fall of New Orleans will cause bad results. If they mass their whole force on the Mississippi now, they will divide our states in half.

Wallwood—Vicksburg, friend, spoils this plan. You will see that they will cut their teeth at Vicksburg.

Westerlaw—It was a hard blow to our cause, that we lost Maryland, Missouri and Kentucky.

Wallwood—Maryland would have been captured by the first onset; it is too thinly populated. Those devils, the Germans, have taken Missouri from us, and Kentucky wavered so long in its neutrality, siding first with our, then with the other side, until our enemies managed to gain control. I know that scoundrel Walker, who undoubtedly carries part of the blame.

Westerlaw—What plan has Davis now?

Wallwood—His plan is a good one to my knowledge. McClellan with 120,000 men is at Yorktown. He must be annihilated. That will open the way to Maryland, Washington and Pennsylvania. This is the plan, which Lee is to carry out.

Westerlaw—It is a good plan, and Lee is the right man to carry it out. There remains but the main task of how to annihilate these 120,000 men.

Wallwood—I advised Davis to let nothing remain undone. All forces must be put to work. Our friends in the East and West must be aroused, be it with gold or be it with promises. Bands must be organized to burn down the cities. The Yankees must be terrorized. Then will our hands be free. And believe me, England and France are only awaiting a decisive blow to be struck by us, when they will recognize us. If we will be able to do this, we will be masters of the situation, and we will dictate the law.

Westerlaw—Our ambassadors, whom that Yankee Wilson captured on board a British ship, were given up to England by Seward.

Wallwood—That's just it; that's what I regret. I huzzaed when I heard that they were captured, and hoped that their release would be refused.

Westerlaw—How so? Are Mason and Slidell your enemies?

Wallwood—On the contrary, they are my friends.

Westerlaw—And still you wished that they remain prisoners? I do not understand you.

Wallwood—I wished it, because England would become embroiled with these Yankees on account of the insult offered to their flag. This would be more welcome than recognition to us.

Westerlaw—I do not believe that anything serious would have been the outcome. It would have rained words, for England is renowned for that. Old Bull might have rattled with his sword, but hardly would he have drawn it, for it is hard to embroil that mercenary race.

Wallwood—Let it go at that. Who knows but that France might not have taken a hand. For, believe me, these speculative Yankees are a thorn in the eye of Napoleon, as well as in the eye of greedy England. They are befriended to us because we are no haberdashers, and they also need our cotton.

Westerlaw—Yes; there should be a great scarcity of it in both countries, since its export has been hemmed.

Wallwood—That's it. And that is the cause of the great rise in its price.

Westerlaw—We have a surplus. But this damned blockade!

Wallwood—Yes, I am glad that my ship got safely through, and is safe on the high seas. You know, my "Floyd." The cargo will bring a nice little sum, don't you think so?

Westerlaw—I wish you luck.

Wallwood—You know, the cargo; what do you think it might bring?

Westerlaw—As I know the price fairly well, it will be an easy matter to figure it out.

Wallwood—And out there they pay in gold, which is advancing daily here.

Westerlaw—Yes, it is becoming scarce, and those who have any hold to it.

Wallwood—I want to make you a proposition. I always like to make a deal, and I am also short of money just now. I have loaned too much of it to the government. Purchase the ship as well as its cargo from me. You will find me cheap.

Westerlaw—I will not enter into any business transaction just now. I have another plan.

Wallwood—You will be sure to find me cheap.

Westerlaw—As I said before, I will not enter into any business transactions whatsoever.

Wallwood (*urging him*)—Well, then, participate as a partner; we will share the profits as well as the losses, share and share alike. Give me your hand, and we will make out the necessary papers.

Westerlaw—I must also decline this. As I have said before, I have another plan.

Wallwood (*to himself*)—Damn it! I am lost!

Westerlaw—The cause of my visit is, as you would have it, a matter of business. I have taken a large contract for supplies for the army. The contract is good, and will undoubtedly pay its owner. There is much work, which one cannot entrust to strangers. A partner would reduce the profits. I have, therefore, decided to wed. My wife can oversee house and plantation and the magazines, while I give my undivided attention to the business.

Wallwood—You are proceeding in the right course, if you make a good choice.

Westerlaw—I have reviewed my entire feminine acquaintance, and have decided upon your daughter.

Wallwood—Upon my daughter?

Westerlaw—Yes, and I have come to get your opinion.

Wallwood—I feel myself highly honored. You are a rich man, and I see no objection to yourself.

Westerlaw—Then let us bring the matter to a climax at once, for my time is valuable.

Wallwood—Just as you wish. Hm, my daughter will undoubtedly act coy. You know how girls will act. A bit of romance is also upon her mind.

Westerlaw—That is a small matter, for she will not so easily refuse a man like myself.

Wallwood—I would not advise her to do so. Marie! Marie!

Westerlaw—She knows me and my possessions as well as you do.

Wallwood—Who should not know the rich Westerlaw?

Scene VI.—Enter Marie.

Marie—Did you call me, father?

Wallwood—Here! Mr. Westerlaw!

Marie (*dropping a curtsy*)—May you be welcome.

Westerlaw—My young lady, I take pleasure of assuring you of my esteem.

Wallwood—The gentleman has paid us a visit, and wishes a word with you.

Marie—With me? I do not know——

Westerlaw—I flatter myself, that my possessions as well as myself are not unknown to you.

Marie—We see each other often; you can almost be considered one of our neighbors.

Westerlaw—You do not catch my meaning; I would, that we should become more intimately acquainted.

Marie—I do not know on what account you should wish it.

Westerlaw—Maybe the greatest, the most ardent, if you would allow.

Wallwood—I always like the shortest way. To be plain, Mr. Westerlaw is here to ask for your hand, which I have promised him.

Marie—You cannot do that, for this hand is not free. Mr. Westerlaw, my father likes the shortest way. I will also be plain. I must refuse your proposal, honorable as it is, for I am already a bride.

Wallwood—That's a damn lie! You are not a bride! Did I give my word?

Marie—I did! In the presence of God!

Wallwood—Here stands the bridegroom, otherwise, damn it!

Marie—With your permission I gave my heart to the man you now hate, because he would not allow you to make a traitor of him. Out of revenge, you broke your word. What did the happiness of your child signify to you? I do not complain; not a tear shows you my sorrow, for that tear would delight you; my complaints be but fuel for your hate. No love entreats you for this man to whom this heart belongs. But I swear it, that you shall not bind me to any other!

Wallwood—You defy me on account of that scoundrel?

Marie—On account of the man whom you now hate, because he wanted to hinder you from drawing your country, your people, into ruin. For that honorable man, who, forgetting his happiness, reminded me of the duties of childhood, that I, by God, am now sorry I fulfilled.

Wallwood (*drawing a dagger*)—You damned——

Marie—Here is my heart! Strike! You will not miss it! The love of a father will be no obstacle! Strike! You do not frighten me!

Westerlaw—Matters are becoming uncomfortable.

Marie—Mr. Westerlaw, I will let it with you; if, after what you have heard, you will still persist in your demand, will it be consistent with your honor, with your character?

Wallwood—By the devil! You shall obey!

Westerlaw—You may thank the dress of a lady that I did not hear that. A gentlemen must have some regard for the sex. Adieu, Mr. Wallwood, I will undoubtedly find another bride. (*Starts to go.*)

Wallwood—Hold! Westerlaw! Hold! She must consent! Hold, I say!

Marie—God give me strength to bear it! [*Exit into next room.*

CHANGE.—Same as First Act.

SCENE VII.—Sally and Ball.

Sally—Come here, child; don't be afraid; here we are safe.

Ball—Don't you hear how they are shooting?

Sally—Yes; God protect our people!

Ball—Mother Sally, why are they shooting?

Sally—A band of guerillas has entered the State. They practice murder and destruction, and every other vice.

Ball—What kind of people are they?

Sally—An army of thieves and murderers. They have fallen upon our neighbor, and practice every known cruelty. Frank, who was in the field with the horses, came riding like the wind and brought the news. Our master aroused his men and hurried over there; they are now fighting with them.

Ball—Why don't they whip such people?

Sally—The lash is not intended for them; for them grows wood and hemp.

Ball—Do they hurt more?

Sally—It works better with them anyway.

Ball—Why did these people come here?

Sally—To steal, to murder, to burn down our houses.

Ball—Did we hurt them in any way?

Sally—No. But what do they ask, who often do not spare their own friends.

Ball—O, that is wrong! I will tell Mr. Walker not to allow it.

Sally—He and his son are there with our people to punish them.

Ball—Is my father and William there also?

Sally—Yes.

Ball—They will, no doubt, defeat them.

Sally—May God ordain it!

Ball—Has my father such a gun, like those soldiers on the picture inside?

Sally—Yes; the master has armed them.

Ball—Father must keep that gun, so that I may learn to shoot. When I am a man, I want to be a soldier.

Sally—Poor child, you cannot do that.

Ball—I cannot do that? Will I not soon become a man?

Sally—You will become a man without being free. You were born to be a slave.

Ball—That's bad; I would rather be a soldier. Mother Sally, couldn't you have arranged it, that I would have been born a soldier?

Sally—No; for that, you would have to have a white skin like our master. God made you black, consequently you must be a slave.

Ball—God could have also made me white; he might have known that otherwise I could not have been a soldier.

Sally—Be quiet, my child, what God does is well. Listen! Voices! They are coming nearer! Come in, and let us pray to God, that he protect our people.

Ball—If I could only fight with them; I would shoot them all down! [*Exit both.*

Scene VIII.—Walker; Slaves; Stevens.

Walker—Well, that band of robbers is broken up; my son and the others are pursuing the fugitives. William, you are wounded; I will send for the doctor.

William (*whose head is bound up*)—Not necessary, master; the wound is not dangerous and will heal up of itself.

Walker—With this wound you have saved my life. All of you have acted like men. Already, my son and I were surrounded by this gang of cut-throats. You cut your way through to us and made us victors. Stay as long as you wish with me, but if you would try your fortune elsewhere, go, with God, I make you free.

Negroes—Free! Hurrah! Three cheers for Mr. Walker! Hurrah! Hurrah! Hurrah!

Prisoner—Mr. Walker, you are a gentleman. I am also the owner of a plantation like you. War often mixes us up with matters, in which we do not always agree. He, who once joins a cause, has not to wish, but to obey. Nor can the individual be made responsible for the deed, that the whole demands. Therefore, give me also my freedom.

Walker—You free? Wretch! Had you been a soldier, captured in open warfare, you would find protection in this house. Now, you are but a thief, incendiary and murderer. You fall upon the unarmed, spare neither wife nor child. The weak, old man you strike down, only to cool your thirst for blood. You are not bound by any oath to support your flag; you do not recognize any command. You do not fight for principle; you destroy. And murder but to kill, to steal. Your shame be upon you; and shame be upon the government, which allows such a fiendish proceeding. Were I not as human as I am, by God, you would already be suspended between heaven and earth. But still, in the scoundrel, in the murderer, do I honor the man, and allow the law to pursue its course. Boys, guard him, while I make out my report. I will turn him over to the military court.

William—Well, boys, we are free! My chest would burst at the thought. My wish has been granted, by God. Now, mother, you have a happy child!

Negroes—We always fared well under our master, but, still, liberty is better yet!

Scene IX.—Enter Sally.

Sally—O, God! William, you are wounded!

William—I feel nothing of my wound! Mother, we are free!

Sally—Free?

Negroes—Yes; William has saved the master's life by this wound, and for this our master has set us free.

Sally—William! You did this?

Negroes—Yes; William through himself between, as yonder man tried to split the master's head. (*Pointing to prisoner.*)

Sally—God be praised, that He allowed you to do it!

Turns to prisoner and utters a shriek. All stand surprised.

Sally—Stevens! Do you remember me?

Stevens—You know my name?

Sally—Do you remember that negro girl Sally, whose father you whipped to death? Don't you see his bloody corpse under your lash?

Prisoner (*terrified*)—Sally!

Sally—Do you not see my crazy mother on the burning roof? Do you not hear her curse: "As true as this house, destroyed by the flames, will crumble to ashes, so true, if there be a just God in heaven, will you fall as a victim at the hands of my child." God is just! He himself leads you to judgment. (*She grasps one of the negro's guns.*)

William—Mother, what are you doing?

Sally—What God commands! (*Shoots the prisoner, who falls to the ground.*)

Scene X.—Enter Walker.

Walker—What is the matter? (*Espies the prisoner.*) Ha! Who did this?

Sally (*raising her right hand, calmly,*)—God! Through this hand!

Curtain.

ACT III.

Scene I.—Same as Act II. ; Wallwood's House.

Ben (*sneaking into room*)—Something is going on here, and I must know what it is! By the devil, I must know what it is. The master is going around with a triumphant look; it is as if hell was written upon his grinning face. His daughter, for the first time in years, has such a joyful air; her eyes are sparkling with joy. What is going on here? I must know, if joy would again make its home here, and if so, I must try to scare it away. Their sorrow is my only comfort. Still, the daughter is kind; I believe, I could bear it to see her happy. But he, that devil, who bought me! He, who, laughing, tore me away from my wife, to him shall joy remain unknown on this earth! Could I but hear them! (*Listens at the door.*) I must see what's going on; I can't hear a word; even in their joy they do not forget their caution. Listen! They are moving their chairs. [*Exit hurriedly through the centre.*

Scene II.—Wallwood ; Marie.

Marie—Who would have thought it; I am still in a dream!

Wallwood—The messenger has gone long ago; you wrote him not to let us wait, did you not?

Marie—Don't be uneasy; his heart commands dispatch. But tell me, dear father, what good spirit has come over you, that has changed you so? When I saw you today, so kind, as I have never before seen you, so loving and friendly, it seemed to me as if you were mocking my heart—as if it were cruelty, which insulted my grief.

Wallwood—You will soon be convinced of something better.

Marie—I am that now, for you have again given your consent to my happiness. On your wish did I write to my George. I feel ashamed, that I have been so cold, yes, even disobedient to you. But, now all will be changed; I will divide my love between yourself and George.

Wallwood—Yes, yes; it will find itself.

Marie—But tell me, dear father, what caused this change? To me my joy is so doubtful, so surprising.

Wallwood—You know, our cause will undoubtedly fail, and there remains but little hope. Thereupon, I thought it would be better that we made peace.

Marie—Peace? Yes; peace! May God grant it!

Wallwood—And above all, I wanted to reconcile you.

Marie—You will see at my love, that you have a thankful daughter.

Wallwood—You wrote him that he should come alone, so as not to attract attention, did you not?

Marie—Yes, I wrote him; but, dear father, we will go with him; we will remove to Kentucky, won't we. You are poor, as you have often told me. That matters nothing, as George has enough to provide for both of us. Old Mr. Walker, I guarantee you, will be glad to have you.

Wallwood—I believe it.

Marie—You are so cold, while my heart is nearly bursting with joy.

Wallwood—With me it is internally.

Marie—And how came you to know that George is serving with this corps?

Wallwood—I saw him myself.

Marie (*joyously*)—How? You have spoken to him?

Wallwood—Not exactly; I saw him at a distance.

Marie—Oh! Had you but spoken with him, he would have been pleased to know that you are so changed. How heartily would he have embraced you!

Wallwood—I wanted to defer it until later.

Marie—That you disagreed with him at that time will be forgotten when you give him your hand; I know his heart.

Wallwood—I will give him my hand, you may depend upon it.

Marie—I wrote him that you now see your error, that you now feel that he was right at that time.

Wallwood—Certainly; he was right!

Marie—O, God, how happy I am! How happily we will now live! How easy it will be for me to cheer up both you and Mr. Walker, and brighten your old age!

Wallwood—If he will only come.

Marie—He will come! He will come! My heart tells me so! But why did we not go to meet him? In my joyfulness I did not think of it! Why are we here yet? Come; let us hurry!

Wallwood—I first wanted to be convinced of his opinion.

Marie—I will guarantee for that. God! I do but now remember, that he is in the enemy's country! He comes alone! If an accident should befall him?

Wallwood—Be quiet! Our troops are far away, while his corps is but a few miles from here.

Marie—I had not thought of that; what would be an easy matter for us, is a difficult one for him. O, this anxiety will kill me!

Wallwood—You are a woman, who sees ghosts everywhere.

Marie—O, let us hurry to meet him; we have fast horses; we can be there before he leaves the camp.

Wallwood—Why not? That would make a nice mess!

Marie—And why? We are known throughout this region; no one will dare to stop us. And where George stands, we will be safe.

Wallwood—That may be so, but how would we get back? And much remains here to be done. You will leave with him immediately; I will follow later; that will be better. Just let him come.

Marie—Dear father, I would not like to hurt your feelings with my fear, especially today, when you are making me so happy. But cannot I allay my fears, while the thought that my note may prove his destruction, is incessantly on my mind.

Wallwood—Were he only here; you would soon be quieted. Hm, did you in your note hint, that we might return with him?

Marie—I wrote that I hoped that our united loves might coax you to accompany us.

Wallwood—That was good! That ought to bring him!

Marie—Dear father, let us go to meet him.

Wallwood—That's impossible! Don't bother me any more!

Marie—God forbid that I should bother you, now, where you are such a dear, good father. And, so as not to call your displeasure down on me, through my fears, I will go into the corner room, where I can see a long stretch of the road. I will not step under your eyes again until I can see my George in your arms. Adieu, my dear, dear father! How happy I am in your own and his love. [*Exit through centre.*

Wallwood (*alone*)—Go! You will soon be convinced of my love! If he is as easily fooled as you are, my plan will be successful. I wonder, if I should tell her now that I am not her father; that she was born before I learned to know her mother! And that only on account of her mother's wealth did I consent to cover her dishonor with my name. Until now the secret was imperative, for otherwise she might have appeared as the rightful heir. But now, since I am poor, this cause is unfounded. No one but her aunt knows of this matter, and her silence I have secured by a terrible oath. Hm! Hold! Would it not be better to keep the secret a while longer? If that scoundrel is put out of the way, all hope will die within her breast, and with it her will. She will then be a toy in her father's hand, and will be easily led by him. I will then be able to force her to marry that rich Westerlaw, and then I will be able to rehabiliate myself with his money. If I were to disclose the secret, I would myself sever the ties by which she holds herself bound to me. She would then plot for revenge of the murder of her love and herself become a menace to me, for she is very firm of purpose. (*Loads a pistol.*) Above all, we must prepare ourselves for the reception. One does not know how he will appear; such a thing as this comes handy in case of emergency. 'Twas against my plan, if I could rely on my other help.

SCENE III.—Enter Ben.

Wallwood (*hides the weapon*)—What do you want here?

Ben—A stranger wishes to speak to you, master.

Wallwood—Hm! Bid him enter.

Ben—Yes, master. [*Exit.*

Wallwood—Can it be him? It is hard to believe that she has not seen him.

SCENE IV.—Enter Stranger.

Wallwood (*for himself*)—A strange face! (*Aloud*) You wish to see me?

Stranger—If you are Mr. Wallwood.

Wallwood—I am, and what do you wish? But, be seated! Above all, I would like to know your name?

Stranger—That has nothing to do with the case. In matters like mine, it is not always safe to carry your name on the tip of your tongue.

Wallwood—Strange; to satisfy you, I can assure you, that we are alone.

Stranger—That is well; but in regards to the name it matters nothing.

Wallwood—Well, then, proceed!

Stranger—You have corresponded with a young man in Washington?

Wallwood—Who told you so?

Stranger—He himself; he showed me your letters, that I might read them.

Wallwood—Then you are an intimate friend of his, and refuse to let me, his most intimate friend, know your name.

Stranger—That may come, when we learn to know each other better. It is a matter of principle with me, not to give my name in such matters. But I have news that might be of some interest to yourself.

Wallwood—And that should be?

Stranger—On the 8th inst., Lincoln was re-elected for the second term as Presipent of the United States.

Wallwood (*jumping up*)—Damn it! Are you sure that you have reliable information?

Stranger—With my own eyes; in every paper.

Wallwood—Are you from Washington?

Stranger—From Baltimore.

Wallwood—How did you manage to get through the lines?

Stranger—That's a mere nothing when you deal with people like myself.

Wallwood—I do not yet know the reason of your coming here, as I cannot well accept the re-election of Lincoln as the same.

Stranger—Last year I was hired by your agent in New York, and during the riots from July 13th to 17th I did what I could.

Wallwood—Alas, the object in view was not attained.

Stranger—When all was lost, I had to flee; I was not pursued, as no one knew my name. You see, how necessary such caution is? I went to Washington, where I found your agent. Through him I became acquainted with Booth, and became so intimate with him, that he allowed me to read your letters. He tried to enlist me to support an important plan, which, as he told me, he had spoken about to you in Richmond.

Wallwood—Hm, Booth, have you nothing in writing from him?

Stranger—Do you take me for such a blockhead to carry such important documents around with me? And you may depend on my word, Booth is the right man for your undertaking.

Wallwood—Do you think so?

Stranger—And the late election demands the undertaking.

Wallwood—Certainly! Certainly! You say that Booth is the right man? What does he want of you?

Stranger—Hm, there is more to do; there are still more on the list.

Wallwood—I see you are initiated. There is no further use for caution.

Stranger—Booth is watching like a lynx for his chance, and does not allow his victim to get out of his sight.

Wallwood—And did he not entrust you with a verbal message?

Stranger—Nothing more than that he would keep his word as a man.

Wallwood—Enough! Enough! And you——

Stranger—I wanted to convince myself above all what the affair might bring.

Wallwood—You may believe——

Stranger—In a case like this, I believe only what I see. I am not a crank like my friend Booth, but prefer to see my way clear. First the price, then the work. You then know for what you are carrying your hide to the market.

Wallwood—You may be assured of the highest reward.

Stranger—Those are the words of your agent; if I wanted to depend upon them, I would have spared the trip hither.

Wallwood—I swear that you——

Stranger—I have sworn the oath of allegiance to the Union no less than three times, and you don't think that I will trust your oath any more than my own.

Wallwood—How do you mean? You don't expect us to pay you in advance?

Stranger—That is more than I expect. But you deposit $40,000 in the Bank of England, and send the papers to your agent. He then, in my presence, delivers them to a mutual friend in Canada, and they belong to me when the deed is done.

Wallwood—Hm, hm. Think of the sum!

Stranger—Does it seem too high for my head?

Wallwood—Did you not in New York——

Stranger—That was different! There were a thousand avenues open for escape. The whole affair did not bring me over $500. But against what Booth intends to do now, it was mere child's play.

Wallwood—But, remember the circumstances! Remember the blockade!

Stranger—That is very simple. You go direct to your enemies, and give out that you are a fleeing Unionist, and swear the oath of fealty. Then proceed to New York or Baltimore, and from either point you can safely ship the money to Europe.

Wallwood—There we will have to pay in gold?

Stranger—That's understood! Or, do you think that I would risk my head for that paper money of yours?

Wallwood—That will be a too roundabout way of proceeding, and takes too much time. I should think, that if the Government Bank at Richmond guarantees the amount, that it will be as safe as in London. Besides, when you have fulfilled your contract, you will most likely flee in this direction, won't you? For where would you be safer?

Stranger—That is not certain. The way to Canada is free from soldiers.

Wallwood—We must go to Richmond to conclude this matter, as I am not able to do it myself.

Stranger—Let us loose no time, then.

Wallwood—Hold! Hold! I have a little job to do here; why, Hell, I can use your assistance.

Stranger—And for what?

Wallwood—Well, listen! I have a daughter. But, listen! A carriage! (*Hurries to window.*) Yes; that's friend Westerlaw; but he comes all alone!

Stranger—What sort of a man is he?

Wallwood—My friend and confederate.

Stranger—If he is not actively engaged in this matter, I pray you, not to speak of our agreement.

Wallwood—If you wish it; but there is no danger.

Stranger—The less people know of this, the better the secret will be kept.

Wallwood—Enough! Enough! But still!

SCENE V.—Enter Westerlaw.

Wallwood—Welcome, welcome, friend. But why alone?

Westerlaw—Mr. Wheeler is traveling; my overseer is sick; and so I was the only one left that was invited.

Wallwood—Good; as through accident, we have another friend here.

Westerlaw—Whom do I greet in this gentleman?

Wallwood—This is Mr.——

Stranger (*quickly*)—Johnston; at your service.

Westerlaw—Pleased to meet you. Are you related with our brave Johnston?

Stranger—The General? I would feel highly honored if I were!

Wallwood—Well, friends, listen! Our time is short, and we must come to the point. (*To Westerlaw*): I invited him hither that you might be revenged; upon the man who insulted you.

Westerlaw—And who should that be?

Wallwood—You do not know him and have never seen him.

Westerlaw—And still I should have been insulted by him?

Wallwood—Not by him, but on his account. You will recollect, that while you were courting my daughter, how the disagreeable affair terminated, and that she refused your offer on account of a young man. This man is from Kentucky, a Southerner like we, and is serving as an officer with the Yankees. His father alone is to blame, that his state did not make common cause with us, for he is a damned abolitionist, as well as his son. Now, I was out scouting yesterday, and saw the fellow in uniform with the corps that has taken up its quarters a few miles from here. I, thereupon, planned to get him into mine and your hands. Through seeming acquiescence to her choice, I persuaded my daughter to write him and invite him here, and I am expecting him every minute. For this reason, I asked you to come with your men. For myself alone, it would have been no easy task, as the negroes cannot now be depended upon; those days are past. As luck would have it, this friend has also put in his appearance.

Westerlaw—Yes; but I am unarmed.

Wallwood—There shall be no struggle.

Ben is seen listening at window.

Wallwood—After we have the fellow transported, she will become your wife.

Westerlaw—If it were only over.

Wallwood—We are three against one. I will send the negroes to the fields; we will then be undisturbed.

Westerlaw—What shall we do? One must sacrifice himself for his country——

Stranger (*laughing*)—And for love!

Wallwood (*rising*)—I am going to send off the negroes now.

Ben disappears from the window.

Stranger—Have you heard from him that he will come?

Wallwood—No, the messenger is not back yet; I depend on his love for my daughter.

Stranger—The matter is not certain!

Wallwood—I have good hopes. My daughter is sitting upstairs at the window, and will let us know when he is in sight. Just keep quiet, so that she will notice nothing. I will be back immediately. [*Exit.*

Scene VI.

Westerlaw—Did you come from Richmond, Mr. Johnson?

Stranger—No, sir, from Baltimore. I was scouting.

Westerlaw—Well, what is the latest news?

Stranger—Lots of news, but not very good. Lincoln is re-elected.

Westerlaw—The devil!

Stranger—And the eyes of friend and foe are turned upon Sherman. His march through Georgia——

Wallwood—Do they know in Baltimore what his intentions are?

Stranger—No one knows, but he and Grant; I don't believe that they in Washington, or that his own Generals know it.

Westerlaw—That is just the trouble with this Grant! Before this, we knew the Yankees' plans before they knew them at headquarters, and we could prevent their carrying out. Now all is changed. This throng moves in all directions, and when one thinks their object has been discovered, and prepares to defeat it, the devils are on the other side. Through his manuevering he has been able to hide his real object.

Stranger—That's it. Great things will have to be done to turn the tide in our favor.

Westerlaw—One must not lose hope; we, too, have our armies, and Lee.

Marie's voice on the outside—He comes, father, he comes!

Stranger—What's that?

Westerlaw—The daughter's voice; undoubtedly, the anxiously awaited one is coming.

Stranger—Well, the job will now soon begin.

SCENE VII.—Enter Wallwood.

Wallwood (*hurrying*)—He comes! Now, friends, hurry into this room; I will not let you wait too long. The negroes are out of the way; the enemy is here; now can revenge have full sway!

Westerlaw—Well, come on, Mr. Johnston!

Stranger and Westerlaw go into next room.

Wallwood (*alone*)—Now, friend Walker, the hour has come in which I hope to strike your heart. Ha! How the thought of your despair refreshes me! And that you may know whose hand directed it! I myself did send you the message!

SCENE VIII.—Enter George and Marie.

George's uniform is hid by mantle.

Marie (*entering*)—Father, here is my dear George!

George—Accept my hearty greeting, friend Wallwood. O, how happy I am, to again give you my hand as a friend.

Wallwood—I too! I too! Now make yourself at home; take off your things!

George—The time is too short for that, as our corps will strike camp in a few hours.

Wallwood—Yes, yes; you must strengthen yourself.

George—My dear friend, that is impossible. Some accident might also overtake me, and, though I am among friends, still I am in the enemy's country. By God, only Marie could have induced me to take this step.

Wallwood—She will thank you for it. But now, do me the honor and take off your things; I will stand the consequences.

Marie—Well, then, George, take off your things, and if for a short time only.

Wallwood—We will return with you at once.

Marie—O, you dear, dear father!

George—You mean it; then let me embrace you as my father!

Wallwood—First take off your things.

George—Let it be so, but I pray you hurry (*takes off cloak*).

Wallwood—Certainly! Hm, you are well armed.

George—Remember, I am in the enemy's country.

Wallwood (*removing the pistols*)—Give them to me, and now make yourself at home.

Marie—Come here, George! The love that strengthens the hero shall now disarm him. (*Takes his sword.*)

Wallwood—That's right, my child! (*Hastily takes the sword.*) Now, go and put your things in order.

Marie—That shall be done at once. Friend Cupid shall help me pack. [*Exit.*

Wallwood—These are fine weapons; with these you have undoubtedly brought down many a Southerner.

George—They have been of good service to me.

Wallwood—And they undoubtedly will be in the future. (*Takes weapons into next room.*)

George—Where are you taking them? Why don't you leave them here? One never knows—— (*follows him*).

Wallwood (*hastily re-entering room and slamming door*)—Don't worry! They might be in our way; and now, let us talk. What are your next plans for operation?

George—I do not know. With us, no officer knows what is going on before he receives his instructions.

Wallwood—Yes, yes; Grant is very cautious.

George—That is good. But now, dear father, hurry.

Wallwood—Immediately; but I want to introduce you to a couple of friends.

George—What! You are not alone?

Wallwood—Rest assured; they are just as good Union men as I am. (*Calling*): Come out, my friends.

Westerlaw and Stranger step out of next room.

Wallwood—Mr. Westerlaw! Mr. Johnston! Here stands the hero, whom my daughter has chosen. I hope, you will make friends with each other.

Westerlaw—I have the honor (*holds out his hand*).

Stranger—Pleased to meet you (*holds out his hand*).

George gives each his hand.

Wallwood (*attacks him from the rear and shouts*)—Hold fast!

Stranger and Westerlaw grasp each of his hands with both of theirs.

George—What does this mean?

Wallwood—That is, so one should not overheat himself by struggling.

George—Wallwood! You would——

Wallwood—Of my opinion you shall at once be convinced. Careless fool, do you not remember my oath in Kentucky?

George—You have disgraced the name of father! You have played with the happiness of a life! You have used this holy feeling for this villainy! If you all are not sneaking murderers, give me my weapons and let me fight like a man!

Wallwood—Fight! With you! We will extinguish your love for fighting at once! Outside, on yonder tree, is the place where you can cool your heatedness. (*Throwing a rope over him.*) You shall not die like a man, but end disgracefully at the rope.

George—Ha! You cowardly curs! (*Tries to liberate himself.*)

Westerlaw—Be quick! He is breaking my arm!

SCENE IX.—Enter Marie.

Marie—What is the matter here? Ha! George!

George—A scoundrelly trick of yonder man, whom you till now called father.

Marie—For God's sake, father! You could—— No! No! It is impossible!

Wallwood—Be quiet! I will hang him in front of your window; there you can exchange your vows with him.

Marie—Father, when nature created you, she disgraced herself! Not father, but murderer, is what my heart calls you. With unhallowed hand you have cut asunder the holy tie that bound me with you. And now, you scoundrels, back! You do not know the frenzy of a woman! (*Starts towards them.*)

Wallwood (*drawing his pistol*)—Back! Or this bullet will pierce the fellow's heart! And now, my friends, out with him to yonder tree.

Scene X.—Ben sneaks in, followed by the other negroes.

Marie (*like crazy*)—God! Have you no angels to save us from these devils?

Ben (*takes away Wallwood's pistol*)—Hold, you cur! Not so fast! We have still to settle our accounts!

Marie—God is with us!

Wallwood—You black dog!

Ben (*covering him with pistol*)—Let us first see who pays the reckoning. Brothers, bind the scoundrels!

Negroes bind Westerlaw, Stranger and Wallwood.

Ben—Now, take them outside to the tree, which they intended for him, and build a fire under them, that they will not catch cold.

George—Hold, friends, hold! I thank you for saving my life, but do not disgrace this honorable deed by such cruelty. Tie them together!

The negroes tie them together, back to back.

George—You brave fellows come with me; I will enroll you in my regiment. You can then fight against your oppressors in honest, open warfare, and not with cowardly assassination, like these scoundrels here.

Ben—And shall they go scotfree?

George—They will not escape the gallows. Now, get yourselves horses, and arm yourselves as well as you can. A saddle for my bride!

Ben—This gentleman's carriage (*pointing to Westerlaw*) is standing outside; he may be so kind as to loan it to us.

George—That is for you, Marie. But come, lock up the house, so that these scoundrels cannot do us any more harm. (*Gets his weapons.*)

Ben—But may I not apply the torch?

George—No cruelties! What disgraces these, will not honor us. [*Exit.*

Ben (*sneering*)—Well, I wish you much pleasure, worthy sir! [*Exit.*

Wallwood (*stamping his foot*)—Damn it!—[*Curtain.*

ACT IV.

Scene I.—Camp before Petersburg; Soldiers behind Scenes Singing "Star Spangled Banner."

1st Soldier—They are having a high time over at our neighbors, the 52d.

2d Soldier—How so? What's going on over there?

1st Soldier—The father and bride of their Colonel are here on a visit; I was on guard as they passed.

2d Soldier—I am surprised that they are allowed in camp.

1st Soldier—They had a pass from the Minister's office.

2d Soldier—Ah! Otherwise it would have been a very difficult matter, as Grant is very particular about this.

1st Soldier—Yes, the times are past where ladies come into camp to have dances.

2d Soldier—That was a nice affair; but, thank God, now everything is changed.

1st Soldier—If we only had this damned Petersburg behind us. Time hangs heavy on my hands.

2d Soldier—Yes; it is not exactly agreeable. A soldier's life has no greater drawback than a siege like this.

1st Soldier—And yet it is but a short winter's siege, compared with that of Sebastopol. And the climate there, especially when one comes direct from Africa, as I did.

2d Soldier—From Africa?

1st Soldier—Yes; I served in the Foreign Legion. When we came to France, the war with Russia broke out, and I went through the whole business, until after the taking of Sebastopol, peace was declared. I then served under Garribaldi, and fought in Italy. There was life; it was worth while being a soldier; our entrance into Naples I will never forget.

2d Soldier—You have seen quite a bit of fighting in this world. What countryman are you?

1st Soldier—I am a German.

2d Soldier—You Germans are brave soldiers; no one can deny that.

1st Soldier—The Romans found that out when Hermann defeated them in the Teutoburger Forest, and the same spirit still pervades the nation.

2d Soldier—How did you get here?

1st Soldier—From Italy I went back to Germany, and, as I did not like it there any more, I came to America. Upon the first call to arms I enlisted; and when peace is declared, I am going to Mexico.

2d Soldier—How long have you to serve yet?

1st Soldier—Three months.

2d Soldier—Well, it won't last that long here. Sherman is moving up from Savannah; Sheridan is moving on from the Shenandoah Valley. I don't see how Lee can keep it up much longer. And when we get him out of Petersburg and Richmond, all will be up with him; for those, that have not deserted him yet, will most certainly do so in the open field.

Scene II.—Corporal and Soldiers.

Corporal—Halt! Front! Ground arms! Disband!

Soldiers form pyramids of guns.

1st Soldier—Well, Corporal, any news?

Corporal—A spy has been captured.

1st Soldier—Is that so? Where did you take him?

Corporal—Not far from our ammunition train. That negro soldier, Ben, who was on guard there, discovered him. He tried to capture him, but the fellow was too quick, and cut Ben down just as I came up with the guard. We caught the spy and brought him to headquarters. In one of his pockets he carried a hand grenade, and, as I suppose, wanted to blow up our magazine.

1st Soldier—Well, I guess, he has come to the end of his rope.

Corporal—Yes; they will waste no time with him.

1st Soldier—Something must be going on at the right flank. Reinforcements have been coming in all night.

Corporal—Who knows! Grant sometimes sends the most reinforcements where he least expects to attack the enemy, just to fool them.

1st Soldier—And he has often succeeded in doing so, and Lee don't know now where to distinguish sham from realty.

2d Soldier—And often we are fooled the same way.

Corporal—Well, Jack, have you digested your beans already.

2d Soldier—I can feel every one of them in my stomach now.

Corporal—You must wrap them up in bacon; then they will slide better.

2d Soldier—Bacon? I do not eat it; I am a Jew.

Corporal—O, let those who sit behind the stove keep your religious laws; they were not intended for camp-life.

1st Soldier—Believe him if you will! That fellow will eat a whole hog if he can get it. The farmers in Virginia know that best.

2d Soldier—That's not true! Put a well-roasted goose by the side of the bacon, and you will see that I am a Jew. I will grab the goose.

Corporal—Hm, I guess, we are all that kind of Jews.

1st Soldier—I am not so particular about the fare. I don't deny, that in Italy, the pine-apples tasted better than the turnips do here. There, I preferred to chew figs and dates to the beans and crackers here. But after you've got the whole business into your stomach, it don't matter. But I do miss the wine and whiskey.

2d Soldier—You must go to our suttler; he always has some on hand for the officers.

1st Soldier—If the Rebels would use greenbacks instead of bullets, we could also patronize the suttler.

2d Soldier—I don't think that greenbacks are so plentiful over there, and they can keep their paper money. I've got a whole handful of the stuff in my knapsack, which I intend to keep as a souvenir. I got them from one of the deserters.

1st Soldier—How many deserters came over yesterday?

Corporal—There were 150 in the camp.

1st Soldier—If this keeps on much longer, Lee will be in Petersburg all alone.

Corporal—It is no easy matter now; they keep a strict watch and the individual deserter can hardly get through.

2d Soldier—Then they will come over in companies.

Corporal—Well, the thing cannot go on much longer at this rate.

1st Soldier—I hope to God, it will not. This thing makes one tired. There is where the French are above us. They know how to liven up camp-life.

2d Soldier—How so?

1st Soldier—With play, song and dance. While we were in camp before Sebastopol, we even had theatres. And there are always plenty of pretty girls around.

Corporal—Well, I do not miss them.

1st Soldier—What? Are you already callous to the feeling of love?

Corporal—No; but I have at home my dear wife and two children.

1st Soldier—And you left them?

Corporal—I left them at my country's call.

2d Soldier—Then you have more patriotism than I have; I went on account of the bounty.

1st Soldier—I also went on account of that, but now the suttler has got it.

2d Soldier—I guess, he has the bounty money of nearly half the regiment by this time.

Corporal—I left mine with my wife.

1st Soldier—I suppose then, that you do not belong to the millionaires?

Corporal—I live by the labor of my hands.

1st Soldier—Your wife is undoubtedly not living in luxury.

Corporal—I send her two-thirds of my pay; and the citizens are also doing much.

2d Soldier—Well, if one is dependent on that, it goes pretty hard with him.

Corporal—Not always. I convinced myself when I was on furlough. What don't our brave women all do for the hospitals and prisoners?

1st Soldier—Either of which get nothing of it.

Corporal—That's the worst of the enemy, that he lets the prisoners starve.

1st Soldier—And its against the treaties of all nations.

2d Soldier—Is it so? I could not believe it heretofore?

Corporal—I was present at the last exchange. By God, I thought my heart would stand still at the poor fellows' appearance. (*Drums behind scenes.*) Well, what's the matter now?

1st Soldier—It may be a sally in this direction.

2d Soldier—That would make more noise.

Corporal—Fall in! (*Soldiers take guns and fall into line.*)

Corporal—Attention! Shoulder arms! Left oblique! March!
All march off.

SCENE III.—George; Marie; Walker.

George—Do not be afraid; they are only acting as guards
for the tent in which the court-martial is now being held over
a spy.

Marie—The poor fellow! And what will they do with him?

George—Well, he will be shot.

Marie—Horrible!

George—The safety of the army demands this.

Walker—And in times of war, my child, the price of a
man's life is very low.

Marie—Oh! This terrible war! How much blood has not
already been shed!

George—We hope, that it will not last much longer. My
time of service will soon expire, and still I expect to hear the
glad tidings of peace while I am wearing this coat.

Marie—May God grant it.

George—But let us go from a scene which affects you so.
Let us enjoy the other happiness of our meeting. What made
you take such a long journey at this time of the year?

Walker—I myself advised her to do so. She endeavored to
deceive me with forced gaiety, but I plainly saw that some
secret sorrow was troubling her.

Marie—You were not deceived. You see, George, when last
you took me from my father's house into this camp, I thought
that he, by his foul deeds, had severed all ties between us.
But when you sent me with the negro Mark to your father's
plantation in Kentucky, I had time to think over the matter
during the journey. My father's fate stood before my mind's
eye continually, and yet, if he, driven by exasperation, forgot
the child in me, is he not yet my father? Other doubts were
also worrying me.

George—Be calm, Marie. You did your duty as long as
your father acted like a man, but when he tried to make you
the tool of my assassination, he lost the appellation of father.
He severed all ties between you through that crime. Had I
fallen in open warfare by his hand, you could have forgiven
him, for he would have been my opponent. Now, he has

branded himself as an assassin, and sacrificed his own child to satisfy his passion for blood.

Walker—You are certainly wrong, my child. The father has a claim to love and respect, but his love must awaken the love of the child. He must first fulfill his duty before he can expect obedience from the child. If he then deny the father, he himself extinguishes this name in the heart of the child.

George—Misfortune may better him. After he has gone through this strict school, he may see his error. And, if he came back a new man, by God, I would never forget that you bear his name; we would again find ourselves in your heart.

Marie—O, George!

Walker—Therefore, be calm, my daughter. Let peace be declared, and all will be changed. War makes those enemies, who call themselves brothers in peace; we were one people, and will again be so. But now, my son, we must again depart.

George—To-day! And why so hurriedly?

Walker—This is no stopping-place for Marie. Who knows but that to-day or to-morrow the trouble will commence. Her nerves will not stand a cannonade.

George—Marie, will you leave me so soon?

Marie—My wish has been fulfilled. We have seen you alive and hearty. May God protect you in the future.

George—I must first introduce you to our General; etiquette demands it. No doubt, he will allow me to escort you for a few miles, if you insist on leaving to-day.

Walker—In God's name! We still have a few hours' time.

George—That's lucky! I just remembered that a detachment goes back to-day for rations; we will accompany them.

Walker—Be it so. Now, tend to your business.

George—I will first present you to the General; then I have a few minor matters to attend to. [*Exit all.*

CHANGE.

Scene IV.—Headquarters; General; Adjutant.

General—Has no news from General Sheridan yet arrived?

Adjutant—He is rapidly nearing the Weldon Railroad.

General—If this point is taken, the enemy will have to evacuate or otherwise surrender. Send word to all commanders to hold themselves in readiness. As soon as the enemy is engaged by Sheridan, we will commence the attack all along the line.

Adjutant—Very well, General.

General—Is there anything else?

Adjutant—Nothing important. A spy has been captured, and is now before the court-martial. He is a desperate fellow, and shot the guard who discovered him.

General—The trial will be short; go and attend the same.

Adjutant—Yes, sir.

General (alone)—There lie Petersburg and Richmond, the last props of the Rebels. When they fall, I calculate on submission. It was a long and bloody fight, and many a brave man has fallen. Our time will be recorded with blood on the pages of the book of history.

SCENE V.—Enter Adjutant; George, Marie, Walker, later.

Adjutant—General, Colonel Walker, of the 52d, whose father and bride are paying him a visit, begs leave to present them to you.

General—Father and bride! How came they into camp?

Adjutant—With a pass from the Minister.

General—Bring them to me.

[Exit Adjutant.

General—From the minister! They are undoubtedly people of distinction.

[Enter George, Walker, Marie.

George—General, I beg your pardon for asking for the honor of introducing my father and bride to you.

General—Pleased to meet you! You come from Washington?

Walker—Originally from Kentucky. We came through Washington to obtain permission to see my son.

General—So! Well, young lady, I suppose that camp-life is something new to you. How do you like it?

Marie—It takes my breath when I see all these weapons which are trained upon our countrymen.

General—You are right. The soldier's life is indeed a hard one; especially so, when fate decrees, as does with us, that we are pitted against our own citizens.

Marie—O, our poor country!

General—It is indeed to be pitied. But now, how long will you stay here?

Walker—But one short hour, General.

General—You are right. Matters are not pleasant with us just now, but we hope, it will not be long before we will be at home with our families.

Marie—God grant it!

General—How are matters in Kentucky?

Walker—We have nothing more to fear from the enemy; only some few guerillas are still at large and practice every cruelty.

General—Yes; these bands are the scum of this war. How is it otherwise; has trade picked up any?

Walker—We cannot complain since the Mississippi has been opened. But gold is rising in value every day, and with it the necessaries of life.

General—These usurers, who make the crippled condition of the country serve their own purpose, and who, through their swindling operations, are our worst enemies.

Scene VI.—Enter Adjutant.

Adjutant (*handing over papers*)—From the court-martial.

General (*to the others*)—Excuse me for a moment.

Walker—General, we do not want to intrude here.

George—Still, I have a favor to ask of you, General.

General—Well, speak out, Colonel.

George—I would like to have a four hours' furlough, so as to escort my father and bride for a few miles.

General—I will give you the command of the detachment which goes back for rations. You will then have protection for your dear ones.

George—General, I thank you.

Walker—Accept our thanks for your kindness.

General—Go, with God! Excuse me.

[*Exit George, Marie, Walker.*

General (*reading papers*)—Hm! A dangerous subject! It is well, that he fell into our hands. (*Signs judgment.*) You will take charge of the execution. [*Exit.*

Adjutant—Very well, General. [*Exit.*

Scene VII.—Walker and Marie.

Walker—Here is where we should await him; he will undoubtedly be back soon.

Marie—Could George but go home with us.

Walker—He wishes that as well as I, but it cannot be thought of.

Marie—If he would ask for his release, would it not be granted?

Walker—That's impossible, my child. He has but a short time to serve yet, when he will be mustered out with his regiment.

Marie—And why did he join the army?

Walker—A man of honor dare not refuse when his country calls him. See! How many have left wife and child to do their duty as citizens. Europe is astonished over what America has accomplished. A people that cleared the wilderness and created states; a people that drove the ox before the plow, and were engaged in mercantile pursuits, were in one moment transferred into a vast army. Armies sprang up, the like of which had never been witnessed. Our merchant ships became a fleet of men-of-war, before which even the haughty England trembled.

Drums behind scenes.

Marie—My God! What is that?

Walker—Be quiet, child; it is nothing of importance.

A soldier walks past.

Walker—Eh! What means this alarm?

Soldier—The spy is being led onto the parade ground, where he will be shot.

Marie—O, God! Father, let us go!

Walker—Where? We must await my son here.

Marie—Let us go to his tent.

Walker—And in the meantime he may come here. No, child, we must stay.

Marie—Shall we witness the terrible scene?

Walker—They will only pass here: here they are already.

Scene VIII.—Spy; Guard.

Marie (*cries out*)—O, God, my father! (*Runs towards sol-dier.*) Hold! Hold!

Adjutant (*stepping forward*)—What is the meaning of this?

Walker—It is her father, whom you are leading to execution.

Adjutant—Good heavens!

Marie—My father! Let my father free!

Adjutant—The soldier has no will of his own, when the command is given him.

Marie—I will clasp him to my breast, and will not remove until you have granted my favor.

Wallwood—Marie, you are beseeching for me—for him, who would have annihilated you. That melts the ice around my heart. Leave me, Marie, let my fate fulfill itself. This life has no more pleasures for me. I fought for and will go under with our cause. Live happy. Go to your aunt. Tell her, that I will release her from her oath. She will tell you a secret, that will calm you. Farewell.

Adjutant—Poor child, I cannot delay any longer. Mr. Walker, lead the lady away.

Marie—Not without my father. (*Embraces him.*)

Scene IX.—Enter George.

George—What's the matter here?

Marie—George! Come! Come! Save my father!

George—Your father! (*Sees Wallwood.*)

Marie—You must save him! God called us hither to set him free.

George—Marie, come here to me.

Marie—Nature has given me this place, and I will not forsake it alive.

Scene X.—Enter General.

General—What is going on here?

George—General——

Marie—General? God has sent him! General?

General—What do you wish?

Marie—Him! He, who should die! He is my father!

General—What? The spy?

Marie—O, set him free! By all that is holy, I beseech you. Give the daughter her father.

General—I am a soldier, and as such must do my duty, as painful as the same may be.

Marie (*kneeling before him*)—Here I will lie in the dust at your feet, and clasp your knee, until you grant my request.

General (*signals to Adjutant*)—Do your duty.

Adjutant and Soldiers take the prisoner quietly away.

General—My dear lady, arise.

Marie—Not until you sympathize with my sorrow, and give me my father.

General—My child, what you ask is an impossibility. Not I, but the law sentences him to death.

Marie—He must not die! I will carry his guilt! Through my running away, I prompted him to revenge.

Walker—My poor daughter!

George—Marie, do not deceive yourself with such a pretext.

General—Colonel, you will conduct the lady to the carriage, and escort her through the camp; I will send the detachment after you.

Marie (*believing her father present*)—No! No! I will not leave my father! If you have ever felt the love of a wife, or basked in the smile of your child, then restore the daughter to her father.

General—You torture me. I am a soldier, and still a man. But the law stands above feeling.

Marie (*hysterically*)—If you be woman-born, if you were nourished by a woman's breast, so give me my father. God is merciful, and men cannot be so? By your hereafter, I—— (*starts for her father.*) Ha! (*She turns in the direction in which he has disappeared, and prepares to rush after him. At this moment three shots are heard behind the scenes. She falls fainting on the stage.*)

George—Marie! Marie! She is dying! (*Rushes towards her.*)

Walker—Fright has made her faint. (*Runs to her side and clasps her wrist.*)

General—That is the hardest lot of a soldier, when duty denies us the privilege of being merciful.

Adjutant—General, the sentence has been executed. The delinquent is dead.

General—The law is satisfied, and God will help this poor unfortunate.

FINIS.